Detective Derek

Detective Derek

by Karen Wallace
and Beccy Blake

For Amelia

First published 2007
Evans Brothers Limited
2A Portman Mansions
Chiltern St
London W1U 6NR

British Library Cataloguing in Publication Data

Wallace, Karen
Detective Derek. - (Skylarks)
1. Children's stories
I. Title II. Blake, Beccy
823.9'14[J]

ISBN-13: HB 9780237533885
ISBN-13: PB 9780237534066

Printed in China by WKT Co. Ltd.

Series Editor: Louise John
Design: Robert Walster
Production: Jenny Mulvanny

Contents

Chapter One

Derek was a cat who cared about one thing. He wanted to join the police force and be a detective. After all, said Derek to himself, if dogs can do it, why not cats?

Also, cats don't drool, they don't have stupid barks and they never, ever knock over cups of tea with their tails. In fact, everyone knows that cats are tougher and smarter than dogs. So Derek decided to take action. He put up a big poster in the roughest part of town. The poster said:

WANTED

POLICEMAN

MUST BE TOUGH,

SMART AND LIKE CATS

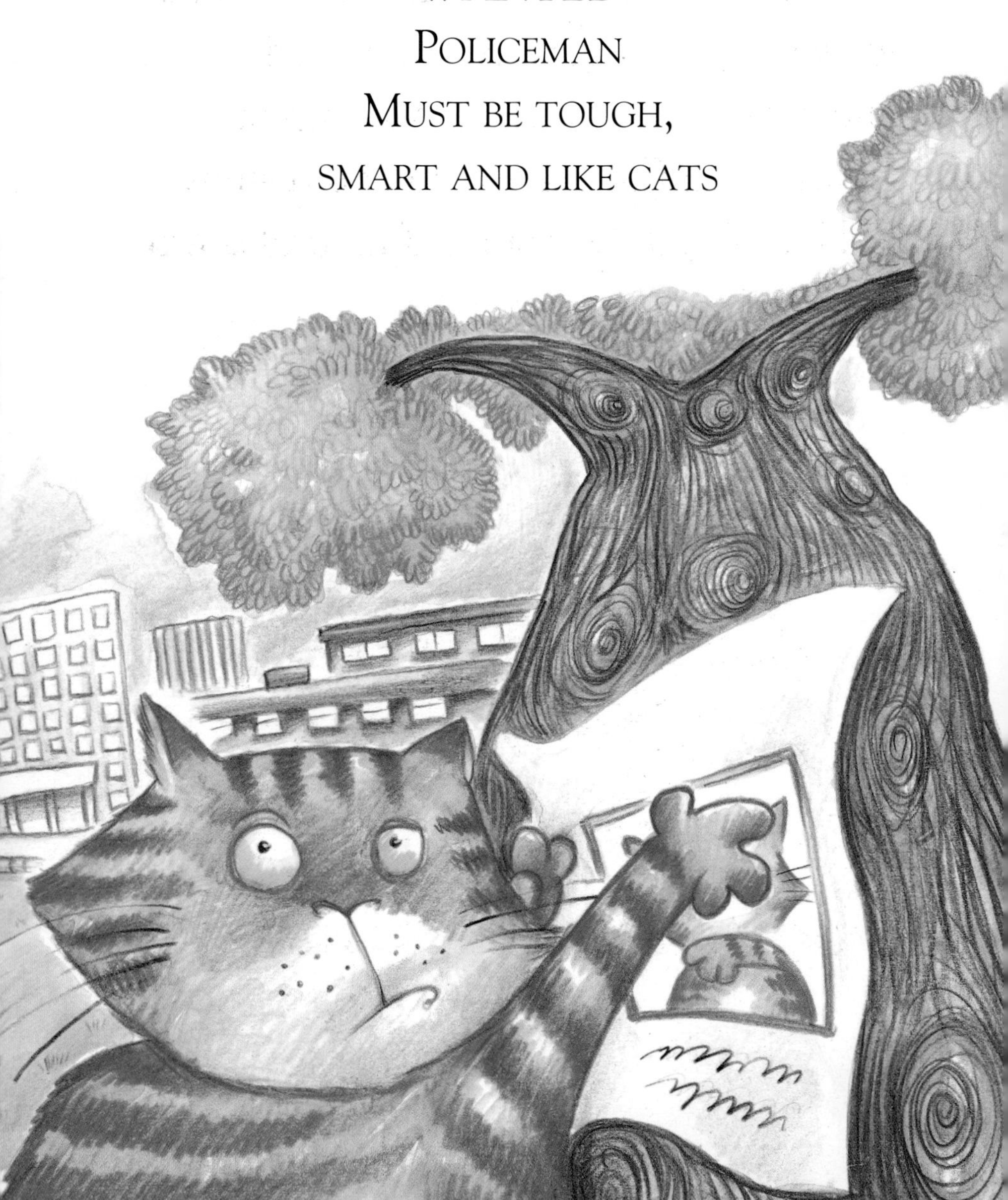

Then Derek hid up a tree, crossed his paws for good luck and waited.

Half an hour later, Sergeant Norman walked by. Sergeant Norman had enormous feet so he could stamp out trouble in a flash. He also had a shiny red ball which he bounced up and down

really fast when he wanted to think really hard.

Sergeant Norman stopped and read the poster.

Derek watched as the shiny red ball went up and down.

"Huh," said Sergeant Norman to himself. "Sounds like a good idea to me. If dogs can do it, why not cats?"

It was exactly what Derek wanted to hear!

He leapt down from his branch and

rubbed his face against Sergeant Norman's ankle.

It was amazing. Sergeant Norman and Derek looked each other in the eye and understood each other right away.

It was as if they had been partners for years!

Sergeant Norman climbed onto his bicycle and Derek climbed onto his back and the two of them pedalled down to the police station immediately.

Chapter Two

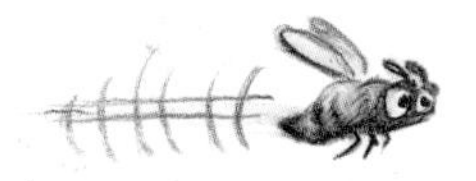

"So you want to be a detective," said Superintendent Sid. He looked into Derek's clever yellow eyes and scratched his head thoughtfully. "That is most unusual. But then again, if dogs can do it, why not cats?"

Derek and Sergeant Norman were both delighted.

It was exactly what they wanted to hear!

"Okay," said Superintendent Sid. "This is the deal. If you two can catch the Mouse and the Boxer, I will make Derek a detective right away."

Sergeant Norman tried not to twitch.

Derek felt his fur stand up on end.

The Mouse and the Boxer were the sneakiest crooks in town. The Mouse was really mean and played nasty tricks on everyone. The Boxer was just plain bad. But worse than that, no one could catch them because they were brilliant at disguises.

Often it was impossible to guess who they were until it was too late. This was going to be a really tough job.

Derek jumped onto Sergeant Norman's shoulder and purred in his ear.

"Don't worry, Superintendent," said Sergeant Norman. "You can rely on us. We'll catch them red-handed and put them in jail."

Superintendent Sid let himself smile which didn't happen often.

"That's what I wanted to hear," he said. "There's just one question."

"What?" said Derek and Sergeant Norman at the same time.

Superintendent Sid leaned forward. "Do you like opera?"

Derek and Sergeant Norman exchanged looks. They understood each other so well, they didn't even have to speak.

I hate opera, thought Derek.

So do I, thought Sergeant Norman.

"Too bad," said Superintendent Sid, who could tell from the look on their faces that opera wasn't their favourite thing. "The Mouse and the Boxer love opera and they particularly love Belinda Bellows."

Derek and Sergeant Norman exchanged looks again.

Who's Belinda Bellows? they wondered.

Superintendent Sid rang a little bell on his desk.

Two policemen walked into the room and held up a poster. It showed a picture of a very large lady with curly blonde hair. She wore diamonds in her hair, diamonds in her ears and diamonds around her neck.

On the poster were the words:

AT THE GLITTERING GARDENS

FOR ONE NIGHT ONLY

BELINDA BELLOWS SINGS

OPERA!

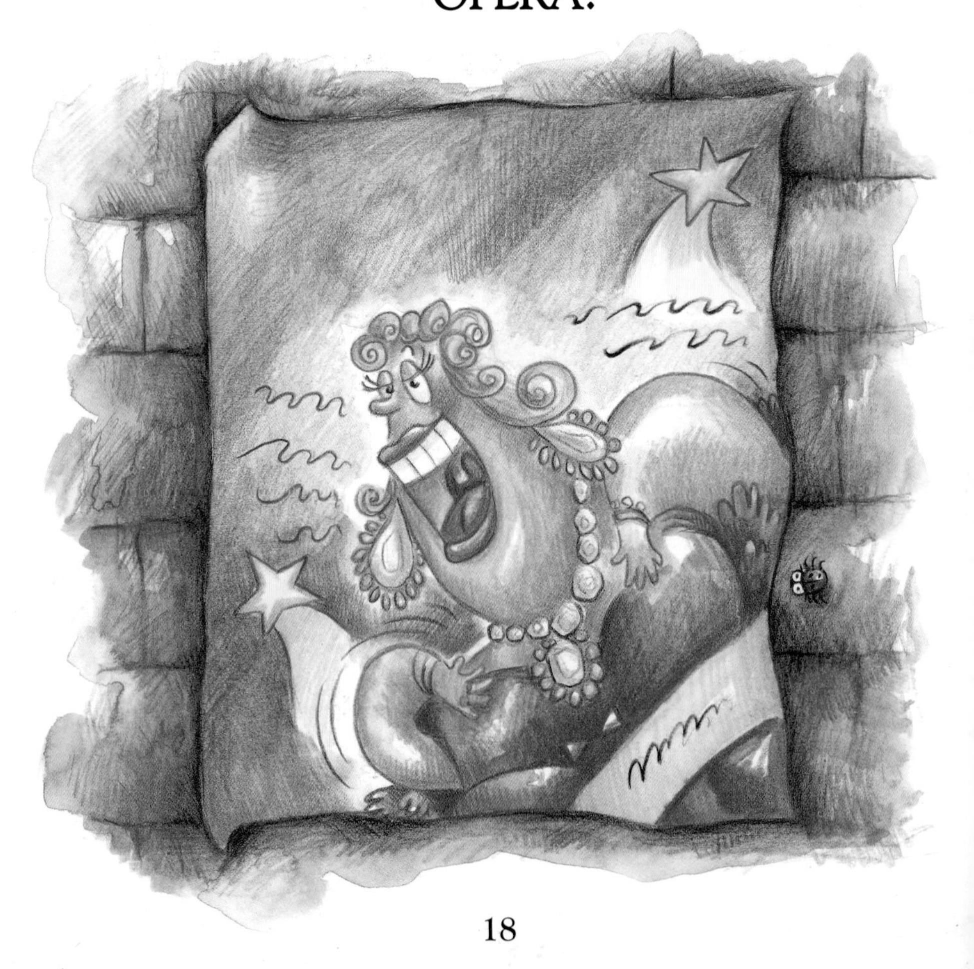

At the bottom it said:

A truly shattering experience – *The Daily Screamer*.

"Belinda Bellows loves diamonds," said Superintendent Sid. "And she loves singing in a really high voice."

Derek and Sergeant Norman looked at each other again.

So what?

Superintendent Sid took a deep breath. "The Mouse and the Boxer love diamonds too, and Rich Rocks Jewellers has a very special tiara and a necklace on show at the moment."

Derek and Sergeant Norman thought hard.

"So you think the Mouse and the Boxer will try to steal the diamonds to impress Belinda Bellows," said Norman.

Derek fixed the superintendent with his clever yellow eyes.

"Yes, I do," replied Superintendent Sid. "And it's your job to catch them red-handed."

He leaned back on his chair. “But what we need most of all is enough proof to put them in jail.”

Chapter Three

Derek and Sergeant Norman stood outside Rich Rocks Jewellers. Sure enough there was an amazing tiara and an incredible necklace in the window.

"The Stars of Paris," said the label beside them. "'Specially guarded

by Crawling Christopher."

"Who's Crawling Christopher?" whispered Sergeant Norman.

But Derek was already inside.

"Crawling Christopher is a fierce, hairy spider," said the manager. "No one could ever steal these diamonds."

He rattled a bag of something called MEATY SPIDER SNACKS.

Sergeant Norman and Derek watched as a great big tarantula jumped from behind the Stars of Paris diamonds and waggled a fierce, hairy leg at them.

"Mmm," said Derek to Sergeant Norman. "He looks pretty frightening, doesn't he?"

But Sergeant Norman was already outside again. He was bouncing his shiny red ball up and down really fast and thinking hard.

A small crowd of people were staring at the diamonds. Mostly they were little old ladies in flowery dresses. Suddenly a huge woman in a nurse's uniform pushed her way up to the front. She had surprisingly meaty arms and wore pink nail polish.

A skinny doctor in a white coat stood beside her. He had a pointed furry nose and little sharp claws on the ends of his fingers.

"I'd never get sick of those," cried the

nurse in a very deep voice. She punched the doctor on the arm. "Sick! Geddit, Doc? Joke!"

The two of them fell about laughing, climbed into an old ambulance and roared off down the street.

Sergeant Norman looked at Derek.

It was the Mouse and the Boxer.

There was no doubt about it!

Chapter Four

"We need a fiendishly clever plan," said Sergeant Norman.

Derek purred. "We take away the real diamonds and put fake ones made out of glass in their place. The Mouse and the Boxer will be sure to steal them and wear them to the opera on Saturday night. And when Belinda Bellows hits the high notes…"

"The glass will shatter and we'll have proof!" cried Sergeant Norman. "Real diamonds would never shatter." He tickled his partner's ears. "Derek! You're a genius!"

"Did I hear you say Belinda Bellows?"

cried the manager. "Why, she's my best customer!" He reached into a drawer and pulled out a fake necklace and tiara. "What's more I have just the thing you're looking for..."

At that moment, Belinda Bellows walked into the shop.

"Show me the Stars of Paris," she sang at the top of her voice. "I want to wear them on Saturday at the Glittering Gardens."

Quick as a flash, Derek swapped the fake diamonds for the real ones in the window. "The trap is set!" he cried. He handed the real diamonds to Belinda.

"Now all we have to do is wait for the Mouse and the Boxer to steal the fake jewels," replied Sergeant Norman.

It didn't take long.

The next morning, Derek and Sergeant Norman were called back to Rich Rocks Jewellers.

"Someone has just stolen the fake diamonds and tied up Crawling Christopher with a pink ribbon," cried the manager.

Sergeant Norman raised an eyebrow. Everyone knew that pink was the Mouse and the Boxer's favourite colour.

Out on the street, Derek saw a very large movie star with long golden hair and surprisingly meaty arms sitting in the back of a pink Rolls Royce.

The driver had two furry ears poking out of his pink cap.

As the Rolls Royce zoomed off down the street, there was a howl of laughter.

Sergeant Norman looked at Derek.

It was the Mouse and the Boxer.

There was no doubt about it!

MB 1

Chapter Five

On Saturday night every seat was taken at the Glittering Gardens. Everyone wanted to hear Belinda Bellows.

Everyone, except Derek and Sergeant Norman. They hated opera. But they had a job to do. They stood high up in the balcony and looked at all the people in the audience through their binoculars.

Everyone was dressed in extraordinarily fancy clothes and everyone was wearing lots of jewels to impress Belinda Bellows.

"I can't see the Mouse or the Boxer

anywhere," said Sergeant Norman.
"Nor can I," said Derek. "They must be wearing extra special cunning disguises." Then suddenly he gasped. "Look down there, three rows from the front."

Sergeant Norman looked.

An enormous woman wearing a tight gold dress, which showed off her surprisingly meaty arms, sat squashed into a narrow seat. On top of her pink curly hair was a glittering tiara. It looked just like the fake one from Rich Rocks Jewellers. Beside her was a skinny figure with a whiskery face wearing a pink velvet dinner jacket. He was fiddling with a diamond necklace fixed to the front.

The necklace looked just like the one from Rich Rocks Jewellers.

Sergeant Norman looked at Derek.

It was the Mouse and the Boxer.

There was no doubt about it!

Now all they had to do was wait for Belinda Bellows to hit the really high

notes and for the glass to break into a thousand pieces.

"What's going on?" asked Superintendent Sid, approaching the detective duo. Unlike most policemen, he actually liked opera and had come to see Belinda Bellows as a special treat. "Is everything under control?"

"Don't worry, Sir," said Sergeant Norman. "Everything is just fine. In fact, any minute now, you are going to have a truly shattering experience!"

At that moment, the curtain rose and Belinda Bellows walked onto the stage.

The Mouse and the Boxer couldn't believe their eyes. How could Belinda Bellows be wearing the Stars of Paris when they were wearing the Stars of Paris?

"Something's up," muttered the Boxer.

"I smell a rat!" squeaked the Mouse. "Let's get out of here, now!"

But when the Mouse and the Boxer stood up, the people behind pushed them down again.

"Sit still!" they shouted. "You're blocking the view!"

High up in their balcony, Sergeant Norman turned to Derek. "Come on!" he cried. "Let's get them!"

Chapter Six

Sergeant Norman and Derek ran down to the stage just as the Mouse and the Boxer squeezed out of their row.

"Not so fast," snarled Derek.

"You'll never catch us now," cried the Boxer and they began to run.

Then something amazing happened. Belinda Bellows hit her highest note ever. KAPOW!

The glass tiara on the Boxer's pink curly hair exploded!

The necklace fixed to the front of the Mouse's velvet jacket broke into a thousand pieces!

All around them, the floor was covered in tiny bits of sparkling, shattered glass.

"It was a trap!" squeaked the Mouse.

"We've had it!" howled the Boxer.

"You are under arrest in the name of the law!" cried Sergeant Norman.

"Those jewels were fake glass diamonds that *you* thieving criminals stole from Rich Rocks Jewellers!"

Click! Clunk! Two pairs of handcuffs snapped around two pairs of wrists.

One pair was thin and furry.

The other pair was thick and hairy.

"Congratulations!" cried Superintendent Sid. He turned to Derek and shook him by the paw. "From now on you shall be called Detective Derek. Welcome to the Police Force."

Detective Derek's heart went bang with joy.

Sergeant Norman was delighted.

It was exactly what they wanted to hear!

"How about a night at the opera?" sang Belinda Bellows. "I'll do it all over

again just for you!"

Sergeant Norman and Detective Derek exchanged looks.

A night at the opera! No thanks! We'd rather go to jail!

Which is exactly what they did.

They put the two nasty crooks into a cage and fixed it to the back of Sergeant Norman's bike. Then Detective Derek jumped onto his partner's back and they pedalled all the way back to the Police Station.

And that is how Sergeant Norman and Detective Derek put the Mouse and the Boxer behind bars for a very long time.

And they never went to the opera ever again!

If you enjoyed this story, why not read another *Skylarks* book?

Spiggy Red
by Penny Dolan and Cinzia Battistel

Spiggy Red is sent to Planet XY73 on his first ever space mission. He must deliver a top secret casket to the famous inventor, Professor Gizmo. Spiggy sets off in his Zooper with great excitement and everything goes well until Spiggy stops at the Lake of the Purple Pong and comes across… the Thing!

Awkward Annie

by Julia Williams and Tim Archbold

How would you like it if people thought you were awkward? Awkward Annie – that's what Mum and Dad call me. I don't think I'm awkward. Not really.

They soon had to change their minds though on the day that Awful Aunt Aggie took us to the park, didn't they? Brave Bella they call me now.

Well, someone had to save the day…

Skylarks titles include:

Awkward Annie
by Julia Williams and Tim Archbold
HB 9780237533847
PB 9780237534028

Sleeping Beauty
by Louise John and Natascia Ugliano
HB 9780237533861
PB 9780237534042

Detective Derek
by Karen Wallace and Beccy Blake
HB 9780237533885
PB 9780237534066

Hurricane Season
by David Orme and Doreen Lang
HB 9780237533892
PB 9780237534073

Spiggy Red
by Penny Dolan and Cinzia Battistel
HB 9780237533854
PB 9780237534035

London's Burning
by Pauline Francis and Alessandro Baldanzi
HB 9780237533878
PB 9780237534059